Presented to

_____

From

_____

Date

_____

Night Light TALES

Andy Holmes

Illustrated by
Tim O'Connor

VICTOR BOOKS

A DIVISION OF SCRIPTURE PRESS PUBLICATIONS INC.
USA CANADA ENGLAND

Dedication

I dedicate this in loving memory to my grandmother, Mrs. Louise Holmes, who went to be with the Lord just four short months before I could give her this book. She never, ever, ever forgot my birthday. And once I grew up and had kids of my own, she never forgot theirs either.

Published in Wheaton, Illinois by Victor Books/SP Publications, Inc., Wheaton, Illinois

ISBN : 1-56476-575-X

Printed in the United States of America

1 2 3 4 5 6 7 — 00 99 98 97 96

Contents

Dear Parent,

First and foremost, this book is supposed to be fun. It isn't a textbook, or a transposed lecture, nor is it meant to be a definitive list of the character traits all good and decent children should have. It's a book that, I hope, will bring a few smiles and chuckles to the young at heart as well as spawn a few light, affectionate or treasured moments between you and your child. After all, that's what books are for.

Andy Holmes

SPECIAL THANKS FROM THE AUTHOR

I realize that most people will not bother reading this. They may feel it offers little, if anything, to their lives. They may be right. Still, there are some who I hope will take the time. Here's a partial list:

Wendy, my very best friend, wife and mother of our children. Thank you for thinking I'm funny (occasionally), talented (always) and worth sharing your life with (most of the time). "There is no other one who makes me feel the way you do. . . ."

My two sons, Shelton (age 5) and Andrew (age 2). Now, I know why God made fathers. You are gifts from heaven and I love you.

My families: Larry, Martha, Matt, Susan, Jeremy, Jason, Shahayla, Mark; Gloria, Tony, Lisa, Tim, Jamie, Connie, Zechariah, Micah, Noah, John, Libby, Marcus, Kacie, Shirley, Gene, Kent, Cassie, Ashley, Taylor, James, Nathalie, Scott, Tonia, Gentry, Haywood & Aileen Neal. Thank you all for stroking my ego on cue and with great patience.

To Jerry and Christy, Kyle, Todd, and the rest of the Educational Publishing Concepts gang. Special thanks to Kyle for untold hours of layout and design. You did a superb job!

To Victor Books/Chariot Family Publishing and, especially, to Liz Duckworth. Thank you for believing I have a voice worth publishing. I am honored to have been given this chance and I thank you in particular for it.

To John Trent: Thanks for taking time out of your overly-packed schedule to review my book. My family is among the *kajillions* taught, inspired and impacted for good through your ministry. Secret thanks to your wife, Cindy, for encouraging me to ask you.

And last but not at all least, to Tim O'Connor. Let me shout it from the housetops: "Your artistry is incredible!" Thank you for bringing these scribblings to life. I could not be more pleased.

CHAPTER ONE:
Faith

I'll never forget an article I read many years ago. It was the feature article of a major publication. The magazine's cover had a picture of a little girl dressed in her Sunday best standing in front of a beautiful, stained-glass window of a church. Big, bold letters blazed the article's title across the front, "Do Kids Need Religion?"

The writer's research and interviews illustrated that even unchurched parents wanted their children to know the stories from the Bible because they felt they would provide a good foundation for the formation of their child's moral character.

Those of us who love Jesus want our children to not only know these stories but to come to know the God they glorify. We want our children to know that God is good, that He loves them, and that He has great plans for their lives. Moreover, we want them to know that God will even turn those things in their lives that are meant for evil into good. I pray these simple stories help your child fall in confident love with the Creator of all.

A Big Sister, A baby, & A basket

"Don't worry, baby," Miriam whispered. "God will make a way for us to stay together. I just know He will." She kissed her baby brother on the head, then left him in the floating basket.

As she hid she saw a beautiful woman step into the river. The woman was a princess— the daughter of the evil King Pharaoh.

15

"Look!" the Egyptian Princess shouted. "There's a baby in this basket! I mustn't let my father find him, or he shall have him killed."

Miriam hurried over to the Princess. "I know a family who will take care of this baby for you," she offered. "May I take him to them?"

"Yes, you may, brave child," the Princess answered. "I will come get him from you once he is older."

As Miriam carried her baby brother
back home, she smiled at him and said,
"See? God did make a way."

Life isn't fair. Good things happen when we don't deserve them. And, certainly, bad things happen to us as well. This classic story beautifully illustrates what the Apostle Paul stated plainly in Romans 8:28: "We know that in everything God works for the good of those who love Him." We are invited to share in the same confidence.

JOSEPH & HIS BROTHERS

"Look brothers!" Joseph shouted. "Isn't it wonderful?" Joseph spun around showing off his brand new coat. "Father just gave it to me!"

"Hmpf!" snorted Simeon. "That's the ugliest coat I've ever seen."

"Me too!" Levi added. "I wouldn't wear that if it were the last coat on earth."

The brothers envied Joseph because he was Father's favorite, and he never stopped bragging about it. Now they were furiously angry about the beautiful coat.

Immediately, Joseph's jealous brothers ripped the coat off his back and threw him into a deep pit.

"Help me, brothers!" Joseph cried. "Please, save me!" But his brothers pretended not to hear. Just then a group of traders came by. Judah had an idea.

"We shouldn't kill Joseph," he said. "Let's sell him to these strangers."

"Good thinking, Judah," his brothers agreed. So they sold their younger brother to the merchants for eight ounces of silver. The merchants took Joseph to Egypt and sold him. He had to work hard as a slave.

In time, Joseph had his share of troubles. He ended up in jail.

But God never forgot Joseph. He gave Joseph a way to help the King of Egypt. The King rewarded Joseph by making him a powerful leader.

Many years later, a
great hunger filled
the land, and
everybody had to
come to Joseph for
their food. One day
Joseph's brothers
came and bowed
down before him.
    "Kind
Master," they
pleaded, not
knowing he was
their long-lost
brother, "please
help us, or we will
starve to death."

PALACE

But Joseph said, "Brothers, it's me!"

"Joseph," his brothers cried, "please forgive us for all the terrible things we did to you."

Joseph kissed them all and said, "Don't
worry, brothers. God took all the bad things
that happened and used them for good."

NOAH

One time God was very sad,
because His people had gone bad.
Everyone did what was wrong,
every day and all day long.

So the Lord made up His mind
to end the world He had designed.
But as He finished making plans,
He found one good and upright man.

His name was Noah and God said,
"I think I'll start again instead."
So God had Noah build a boat
so big you'd think it wouldn't float.

Why so big? I'll tell you true,
that boat became a floating zoo!
Animals from everywhere
came over to the boat in pairs.

Two dogs, two cats, two chimpanzees,
two deer, two cows, two quacking geese,
two grasshoppers, two butterflies,
two birds of every shape and size.

Two elephants, two crocodiles,
two snails (which took a long, long while),
two pigs, two sheep, two peaceful doves,
and many more I can't think of.

Then God said, "Noah,
take your bride
and your sons and
go inside."
Then God began to
send the rain,
till nothing on the
earth remained.

The big boat floated one whole year.
Then God made dry land reappear
and Noah and his family
and all the animals went free.

God marked this day, as you may know,
with a big and bright rainbow.
It's God's promise to all men
that He'll not flood the world again.

Yes, Noah was an
    upright man
whose good life made
    God change His plan.
He served the Lord.
    His faith was strong.
He did right when the
    world did wrong.

Thinking it Over

A Big Sister, A Baby, & A Basket

Why was the Princess afraid for her
father to find the baby?
How did God make a way?
Say this: I WILL TRUST GOD.

Joseph & His Brothers

Why were Joseph's brothers so
mean to him?
What did Joseph say to his
brothers in the end?
Say this: I WILL FORGIVE
WHEN OTHERS
HURT ME.

NOAH

Why was God sad?
What does a rainbow tell us?
Say this: GOD KEEPS
HIS PROMISES.

Chapter Two:
Love, Joy, Peace

I tried to write in such a way as to give this whole chapter a peaceful tone and easy flow. I developed ideas that, I hope, promote a restful, uncomplicated train of thought. I wanted to inspire simple and cuddly images that might nurture feelings of security and calmness in little ones. My prayer is that this chapter might work like a softly sung lullaby in a gently rocking chair.

Take your cue from the Psalmist who wrote:

> O LORD, my heart is not lifted up, my eyes are not raised too high; I do not occupy myself with things too great and too marvelous for me. But I have calmed and quieted my soul, like a child quieted at its mother's breast; like a child that is quieted is my soul.
>
> *(Psalm 13:1–2)*

God's peace is always there, but we have to crawl up in His lap and still ourselves before we can enjoy it.

PSALM 23 FOR LITTLE ONES

The good Shepherd Jesus
loves His little sheep.
He keeps them in His tender care.

He finds them green fields
     where His tired lambs can sleep.
He leads them to rivers so fair.

He makes His lambs
　　　smile.
He makes His lambs
　　　sing.
He fills up their hearts
　　　with His love.

He guides every step.
He is wise and He is true.
He shows them what Heaven's made of.

Through the valley so dark,
  and the danger so near,
His sheep are at peace on His arm.

They know He is strong.
  He will help them along.
They know they will suffer no harm.

He makes them a feast
   in front of the wolf.
He treats them like His honored guests.

Their joy is so great
   as they dine on fine plates,
they feel tingles all over their chests.

His kindness and love
     are theirs every day.
And in His house they will all live.

The good Shepherd Jesus
loves His little sheep.
Oh, the joy our good Shepherd gives!

I love the old hymn that says, "Take from our souls the strain and stress and let our ordered lives confess the beauty of Thy peace." Once that "strain and stress" is lifted, we understand anew how simple the call of God is, how light His burden, how easy His yoke. As Saint Francis discovered so long ago, peace comes from being faithful in the small things. Finding happiness in life is the natural consequence of doing the things God asks us to do with our talents, abilities and responsibilities.

THE ABC's OF BEING HAPPY

Anne the baby Ant asked her Mommy every day, "Why are you so happy?" and she would always say:

"Because I do the things God wants an Ant to do. I work hard all day long, and take good care of you."

B obby the Baboon
asked his Mommy every day,
"Why are you so happy?"
and this is what she'd say:

"Because I do the things
God wants Baboons to do.
I swing from tree to tree
and take good care of you."

Carl the baby calf
asked his Mommy every day,
"Why are you so happy?"
and this is what she'd say:

"Because I do the things
God wants a cow to do.
I share my milk with people
and take good care of you."

Do you want to be happy
like Bobby, Carl, and Anne?
Do what God wants *you* to do,
the very best you can.

We all have fears. Most of the time they are imaginary. Occasionally, we find ourselves in real danger. Either way, God has promised us safety, peace, and divine protection. James 4:8 says, "Draw near to God and God will draw near to you."

SCARY GARY

I heard a scary story
about a scary man,
who had a scary tattoo
upon his scary hand.

He had a scary hairdo.
He drove a scary car.
This is a scary poem.
Are you real scared so far?

They called him "Scary Gary."
Here's what he liked to do:
He'd tiptoe up behind you,
then jump up and scream "Boo!"

Oh, Scary Gary scared me,
though he's just make-believe.
When I first heard his story,
goosebumps climbed up my sleeve.

My eyes bulged out like baseballs.
My knees were shaking too.
I got so scared while listening,
I didn't know what to do.

I nibbled on my fingernails.
I twisted up my hair.
I sat still as a statue.
I tried to disappear!

I hid under my blanket.
I hid under my bed.
I hid off in the corner—
a lamp shade on my head!

I tried to sing or whistle.
I tried to count to three.
I covered both my eyes up,
and sang my ABC's.

I folded both my hands closed.
I squeezed my eyes shut tight.
I got down on my knees then,
and prayed with all my might.

"Dear Jesus, up in Heaven,
I'm trying to be brave.
Please help me know You're with me,
so I won't feel afraid."

Then slowly, very slowly,
I opened up my eyes.
I thought about my Jesus
so big and strong and wise.

And then before I knew it,
my fears all went away.
I know what I'll do next time.
Do you? That's right. I'll pray.

GOD IS THE BEST DADDY

Mommies and
Daddies love babies,
    that's true.

They hold them.
They rock them.
They kiss them lots too.

They clothe them. They feed them.
They help them to grow.
They teach them important things
kids need to know.

God is a Daddy
to each one of us.
He shows His love best
through our Savior Jesus.

He loves us.
He keeps us.
He hears all our prayers.
God is the best Daddy
and He always cares.

Thinking it Over

PSALM 23 FOR LITTLE ONES

What are some ways God takes care of you?

How can we show Jesus we love Him back?

Say this: JESUS LOVES ME VERY MUCH.

A,B,C'S OF BEING HAPPY

What are some things that make you happy?

What are some things that make God happy?

Say this: I WILL HAPPILY OBEY GOD.

Scary Gary

Have you ever felt afraid?
    Tell about it.
What can you do when you
    feel afraid?
Say this: GOD PROTECTS ME.

God is the
Best Daddy

What are some things that you
    especially like about your
    Mommy/Daddy/Parents?
What would your
    Mommy/Daddy/Parents
    do if you got hurt?
Say this: GOD IS MY
    HEAVENLY FATHER
    AND HE LOVES ME.

CHAPTER THREE:
Truthfulness

Ihave a small, but always growing, collection of very old books. I enjoy the peek they give me on the attitudes of the people of the recent past. I'd like to share a paragraph from one of these books. It is titled simply, "Character." It was written by a man named Samuel Smiles and even though the copy I have was published in 1887, it is as timely as ever.

> Truth is the very bond of society, without which it must cease to exist, and dissolve into anarchy and chaos. A household cannot be governed by lying; nor can a nation. Sir Thomas Browne once asked, "Do the devils lie?" "No," was his answer; "for then even hell could not subsist." No considerations can justify the sacrifice of truth, which ought to be sovereign in all the relations of life.
>   Period.

Most, if not all, children go through a season of lying. Many psychologists feel this is a natural part of a child's moral development. Be that as it may, loving parents will want to help guide their child through this season with wisdom and consistency, training their child up to obey God's desire (and gift) of truthfulness. Psalm 51:6 says, "Behold, thou desirest truth in the inward being; therefore teach me wisdom in my secret heart." This twist on a familiar tale rewards confession.

Three Little Kittens

Three little kittens they
lost their mittens,
And they began to lie,
"Oh, mother dear,
We sadly fear
A monster took
our mittens!"

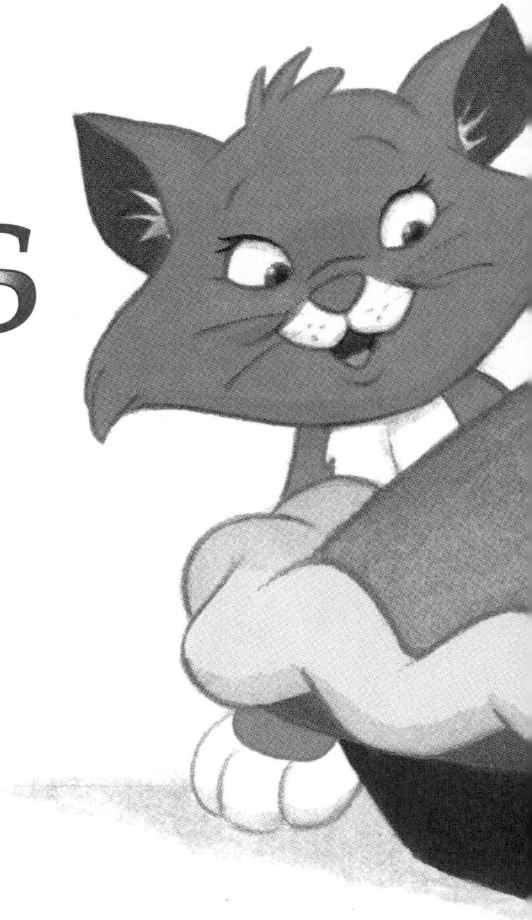

"What! Took your mittens? You poor, sweet kittens
Come in and have some pie.
Mee-ow, mee-ow.
Come in and have some pie."

Three little kitties sat calm and pretty
while they ate the pies.
Then to their fear their gloves appeared
which worried the three kittens.

70

"Why, there's our mittens!" exclaimed the kittens.
"Now that's a big surprise!
Mee-ow, mee-ow.
They weren't the monster's size!"

Three little kittens were sorrow-bitten,
they felt so sad inside.
"Oh, mother dear," they said with tears,
"we really lost our mittens."

"What! Lost your mittens, you truthful kittens,
you've chosen what is wise.
Mee-ow, mee-ow.
You chose truth over lies."

You've probably heard the saying: The road to hell is paved with good intentions. Though this saying may be a bit shortsighted—certainly not an absolute—it does make a worthwhile point. We can be truthful in our intent and yet be made liars when we do not follow through with promised actions. Children seem to be especially vulnerable to missing this correlation. To a child's way of thinking, meaning to do something is often the same as actually doing it. Here's a story to help correct that misconception.

The Boy Who Meant What He Said

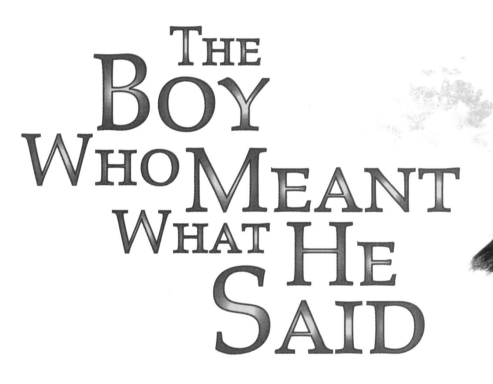

This is the tale of a boy named Ted.
He said what he meant and he meant what he said.
But Ted had a problem as you will soon see.
Listen to this and I'm sure you'll agree.

One day Ted
        said, "I'll
        be back
        really soon,"
but didn't return
        until that
        afternoon.
When his mom
        asked him
        why he stayed
        out all day,
here is exactly
        what Ted had
        to say:

"Well, Mommy, I
        just started
        having such fun.
It took me a long
        time before I
        was done.
I know I said soon
        and that's just
        what I meant.
I didn't lie, Mom.
        It was an
        accident."

The next day Ted's mother
    said, "Please clean the yard."
Ted said, "Okay, Mom! That
    won't be too hard."
Before he got started Ted
    thought it'd be neat
to spend some time playing
    with friends up the street.

Ted never cleaned up
    the yard like he said.
He played and forgot to
    get to it instead.
Again, Ted did not think
    of this as untrue.
It really was something
    that he'd meant to do.

This happened a lot with one thing or another—
with his friends, his dad and, of course, with his mother.
Soon no one believed Ted would do what he said.
They always felt tricked, overlooked, or misled.

Then one day it hit him. Poor Ted understood.
To mean what you say is all fine and good.
But if you don't actually do what you say,
your actions keep truthfulness far, far away.

Now every time Ted says, "I sure will,"
he knows it will not become truthful until
he actually *does* it and that otherwise,
what he meant to be true will soon become lies.

PINOCCHIO NOSE BETTER

Pinocchio's nose grew
    longer with every lie
    he told.
Which gave all those
    around him
    a fun sight to behold.
That is, until Pinocchio
    found miracle
    nose cream,
Which kept his nose
    from growing
    to ridiculous extremes.

Pinoke just had to test it—to see what it would do.
So he told an awful story that was crafty and untrue.
Everyone believed Pinoke no matter what he said,
Even though he'd told them lies he'd made up in his head.

"Amazing!" said
    Pinocchio. "My nose
    stayed the same size."
But soon Pinocchio
    had told a hundred
    other lies.
He almost felt he had to lie
    to keep the last
    lie hidden.
With each new lie he
    told he felt much worse
    and more guilt-ridden.

"I wish I'd never found
    the cream!"
    Pinocchio confessed.
"One lie leads to another lie
    and soon you
    have a mess.
My nose may not be
    growing long enough
    for me to grab it.
But oh," Pinoke admitted,
    "now I've grown a
    lying habit."

Pinoke put down the nose cream and did not use it again.
And very soon his heart became more truthful deep within.
Although his nose would surely grow if he lied like before,
Pinocchio had no desire to tell lies anymore.

The Boy Who Cried "Wolf"
(Or something very much like it)

A shepherd boy out in the field
Cupped his hands and loudly squealed,
"Help! A wolf! Oh, do come quick!
Bring your clubs! Yes, get your sticks!

This wolf is hungry,
    big, and mean!
The biggest wolf I've
    ever seen!
He's gonna eat my
    lambs and me!
Do come before
    I'm history!"

Right away, the
    people came
Not knowing it was
    just a game.
They grabbed their clubs,
    their sticks and rocks
and hurried to protect
    the flocks.

They rushed uphill and
    looked around.
But there was no
    wolf to be found.
The shepherd boy
    laughed hard and loud
and said to each one in
    the crowd,

"There is no wolf. I tricked you all!
I knew you'd come if I'd just call."
He looked at all the sticks and rakes
and laughed until his tummy ached.

But no one else laughed. No, not one.
This wasn't their idea of fun.
They shook their heads and sighed big sighs,
then left and did not say "good-bye."

"Boy, that was great!" the shepherd grinned.
"I think I'll do that trick again.
Help! Help!" he screamed. "Oh do come quick!
Bring your rakes and clubs and sticks!

"This wolf is here for real this time!
And out to do a dreadful crime!
Please come and get this furry creep
before he eats up all my sheep!"

Once again the
people came
not knowing
it was still a
game.
They stopped
their work.
They stopped
their chores.
They raced out to
the field once
more.

"Ha! Ha! I fooled
you all again!
There is no wolf.
It's just pretend!
Oh, what a funny
group of folks
to once again fall
for my joke!"

The shepherd laughed so hard he cried.
His chuckles filled the countryside.
The kind folks shook their heads and then
went back into the town again.

The shepherd watched them walk away
while laughing at the trick he'd played.
But when he turned to check his flock,
he just about went into shock.

For standing there before his eyes
he saw a wolf 'bout twice his size!
"Help!" he shouted. "Please!" he yelped.
"Won't someone please come here and help?"

He yelled till he could yell no more.
He screamed until his voice was sore.
Still no one in the whole town came.
Instead they said, "It's just a game."

The wolf ate all of the boy's sheep,
then wobbled off to rest and sleep.
"It's all my fault," the young boy cried.
"It's all because I lied and lied."

Thinking it Over

THREE LITTLE KITTENS

What really happened to the
    kittens' mittens?
How do you think they felt when
    they finally told the truth?
Say this: I WILL ALWAYS TELL
    THE TRUTH.

THE BOY WHO MEANT
WHAT HE SAID

What did Ned learn about telling
    the truth?
Is meaning to do something the same
    as really doing it?
Say this: I WILL DO WHAT I SAY
    I'LL DO.

PINOCCHIO NOSE BETTER

What does the Bible say about
   telling lies?
What kind of habit did
   Pinocchio grow?
Say this: LIES ALWAYS LEAD
   TO TROUBLE.

THE BOY WHO CRIED "WOLF"

What did the shepherd boy do?
What happened in the end?
Say this: IF I TELL LIES, NO
   ONE WILL BELIEVE ME
   EVEN WHEN I'M
   TELLING THE TRUTH.

Chapter Four:

Self-Control

S elf-control is the root of all virtues. Without it we are slaves to our whims, impulses, and desires. Proverbs 16:32 says, "He who is slow to anger is better than the mighty, and he who rules his spirit than he who takes a city."

Self-control is the means to putting the fork down, turning the TV off, zipping our lips when we're tempted to say something we shouldn't. Self-control can clean up our thought life, help us avoid cavities, and calm down when we feel like exploding. Self-control is our passport to liberty, blessings, and success.

How do we teach it to our children? The same way we are learning it ourselves: through patient, supportive, and consistent repetition and by allowing our children to experience the natural consequences of their actions.

LAZY LENNY

Lazy Lenny
    loved TV.
He watched it
    every day.
He'd rather sit and
    watch TV
than go outside
    and play.

He'd watch TV at breakfast.
He loved all the cartoons.
He'd watch TV at lunchtime
and through the afternoon.

He'd watch TV all evening
and late into the night.
He'd watch and watch and
watch and watch
until the morning light.

It made chore
　　time a bother
as you can
　　plainly see.
He couldn't
　　take his
　　eyes off
that crazy,
　　old TV.

He'd grab the
　　baseball bat
and think it was
　　the broom.
And, oh, what
　　awful damage
he did to that
　　poor room.

He'd try to do his homework
but couldn't concentrate.
His eyes preferred the movie
he had found on Channel Eight.

He'd think he'd grabbed the iron
when he'd really grabbed the cat,
who ripped up all his clothing
in fifteen seconds flat!

And was he hard to talk to?
It's like he had no ears!
Even if you yelled at him,
he still wouldn't hear.

He made a mess at mealtimes.
You'd laugh to see him eat.
Most ev'ry forkful missed his mouth
and landed at his feet.

He had no friends to play with;
that's no surprise to me.
It's hard to know somebody
who is glued to his TV.

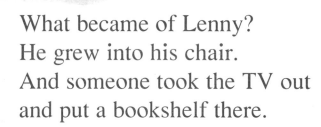

What became of Lenny?
He grew into his chair.
And someone took the TV out
and put a bookshelf there.

107

A Time for Everything

There's a right
time and a
wrong time
for almost
everything.
A time to sit and
read a book,
A time to dance
and sing.

A time to kiss another's face,
A time to be alone,

A time to whisper,
And a time to use a megaphone.

What time is it right now?
I'll tell you straight and true.
It's time to hug the person
who is sitting next to you.

HOLD YOUR TONGUE?

Yakitty
Yakitty
Yak!

Hold your tongue!
Hold your tongue!
Please watch what you say.
Words can hurt people
and cause so much pain.
Be careful with words.
Make them helpful and sweet.
Use kind words with
each person you meet.

113

The mind is a bit of a war zone. Our nature pulls us one way, God's Spirit another. Three things are crucial for our children to understand: First, everyone has ugly thoughts (even grownups); Second, God loves us in spite of them; and, Third, it's easier to "run from" something when you have something to "run to." Philippians 4:8 gives us good counsel: "Finally, my friends, keep your minds on whatever is true, pure, right, holy, friendly, and proper. Don't ever stop thinking about what is truly worthwhile and worthy of praise."

BAD THOUGHTS

Sometimes when I'm angry
I think ugly thoughts.
I don't really mean to.
I know that I should not.

But I'm slowly learning
mean thoughts just don't stay.
When I think some good thoughts,
bad thoughts go away.

A Wayward Young Kid

There once was a wayward
young kid,
Eating candy was all that he did.
Well, he ate and he ate,
till he couldn't sit straight,
and now he's the size of Madrid.

WOW!

WORLD MAP

TOO MUCH CANDY

Candy is dandy and so sweet to lick,
but eating too much of it will make you sick.
Your teeth will turn yellow and full of black dots
which means that your dentist will have to give shots.
And shots are no fun, do I need to say more?
A candy-a-holic has problems galore.

BERNITA BAZZOOM

Did you ever hear of
   Bernita Bazzoom?
The girl who never would
   clean up her room?
She'd scatter her toys
   in hard to reach places
on roof fans, and lamp stands,
   and dusty bookcases.

Used toys, bent books, loose shoes, and her clothes
covered her floor from her foot to her nose.
And when she wanted her favorite dress,
she never could find it in all of the mess.

But perhaps the saddest thing I can recall
was one time at bedtime just after nightfall.
She looked and she looked and she looked for her bed
but ended up sleeping on stuffed dolls instead.

Her mess, like all messes,
   began with one thing,
growing higher and higher with each
   thing she'd fling.

There were skates, rocks, and
   gumdrops and socks worn
   and smelly,
T-shirts and lost skirts and three notes
   from Shellie.

There were marbles and shoestrings
   and doll clothes and Play-Doh.
It looked like a campground for
   training tornadoes!

But such is the price
   messy people must pay
for choosing to not put their
   playthings away.

Thinking it Over

LAZY LENNY

What did Lazy Lenny love to do?
Why did he iron his shirt with a cat?
Say this: TOO MUCH TV IS BAD FOR ME.

A TIME FOR EVERYTHING

Can you think of a time when we should whisper?
Can you think of a time when we can run and shout?
Say this: THERE'S A RIGHT TIME AND A
WRONG TIME FOR ALMOST EVERYTHING.

HOLD YOUR TONGUE

Should we say ugly, hurtful things when we feel angry?
What kind of words should we try to use?
Say this: I WILL SAY KIND AND HELPFUL THINGS.

BERNITA BAZZOOM

What was Bernita's room like?
How did Bernita's room get so messy?
Say this: I WILL PUT THINGS
WHERE THEY BELONG.

Too Much Candy

Dentists help us. How can we help
　　our dentist?

What good habits does our dentist want
　　us to learn? (Brush teeth, eat fruit
　　instead of candy, etc.)

Say this: TOO MANY SWEETS CAN
　　HURT MY TEETH.

Bad Thoughts

How does it make you feel when you　think
　　ugly or hateful thoughts?

What are some good things you can
　　think about?

Say this: I WILL FILL MY MIND
　　WITH GOOD THOUGHTS

A Wayward Young Kid

What is your favorite kind of candy?

What might happen if you ate it all the time?

Say this: TOO MUCH CANDY HURTS
　　MY BODY.

CHAPTER FIVE:

Obedience

Many modern-day "experts" preach a very non-demanding, permissive approach to raising children. However, studies teach us that children often feel unloved in overly lenient families and feel secure and flourish in homes where there are clear, realistic expectations, enforced by consistent, loving, and appropriate discipline. Boundaries provide a sense of security to children.

In this chapter I have tried to convey four perspectives Wendy and I are determined to teach our children. The first is that obedience is for our *protection*. That is, it is there for a practical, beneficial reason. The second is that we should obey *whether we feel like it or not*. Like the once-popular advertising slogan said, "Just do it." Third, obedience *brings blessing*. And finally, obedience (to parents) brings a *special promise from God*.

COTTON FINDS A CAVE

Once upon a time
on a very sunny day
a little lamb named Cotton
found a place to play.

He'd seen this place before
but his mom had told him "No,
this is not a place
a little lamb should go."

Now Cotton was alone
with no one to keep him out,
so he went inside the cave
and began to walk about.

Then he heard a growl,
and suddenly he saw
a hungry bear before him
with big teeth and sharp claws.

He raced back to his mother
and hid behind her knees,
and sighed, "Mom told me no
because she cares for me."

"I don't wanna!" and "I don't feel like it" are familiar phrases to parents. Feelings can be great motivators but must never be allowed to be our master. Here's a classic story about a man who was led astray by his feelings. In the end, he learned a most crucial lesson: Obey whether you feel like it or not.

JONAH AND THE BIG FISH

Jonah raced down the hill toward the row of ships. "Are you sailing to Nineveh?" Jonah yelled to the Captain.

"No, we're going the opposite way. To Tarshish."

"Perfect!" said Jonah. He grabbed his bag, jumped on board and hid down inside the boat's bottom. "God will never find me here," thought Jonah as he drifted off to sleep.

Soon a big storm surrounded the ship, tossing it to and fro.

"Throw everything overboard!" shouted the Captain, "or we're going to sink!"

But the storm grew even stronger.

"Throw me overboard," said Jonah. "This storm has come because I am running away from God. God told me to go to Nineveh, but I don't want to."

Whoooaaoooa!
SPLAASSHH!

GUULLLPPP!

Amazingly, Jonah found himself inside
the belly of a big, big fish.

He began to pray. He prayed and prayed
and prayed and prayed for three whole days. Then all of a
sudden . . .

BLLLAAAWWWKKK!

Jonah was right back where he started.

"Now," said God, "Let's try this again.
Jonah, go to Nineveh and tell them to stop doing bad things, or
I will destroy them."

This time Jonah obeyed God. He walked around Nineveh telling everybody what God had said.

135

Everyone in Nineveh cried and prayed:
"Dear God, we're sorry for
all the bad things we have done.
From now on we will do good things."
        The whole town of Nineveh was saved
because Jonah chose to obey God even when he didn't feel
like it.

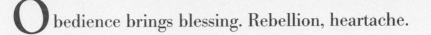
Two Sons

There was a man who had two sons.
We'll look together at each one.
One was a helper. One was not.
One picked the corn. One let it rot.

137

One did his best. One never tried.
One told the truth. One always lied.
One always shared his toys and food.
One was a very stingy dude.

One always tried to do what's right.
One disobeyed from morn to night.
One got a blessing from his dad.
One did not get one. Too bad.

A child should obey his parents because, hopefully, it will be the pathway to a productive life once he grows up. Yet, God doesn't stop there. Instead He adds His personal promise—guarantee—of a rich blessing of a long and happy life to all who heed His wisdom. Just as truly as "the man who loves his wife loves himself" (Ephesians 5:28), the child who honors her Father and mother blesses herself (Ephesians 6:1-3).

Psst. I HAVE A SECRET

Psst. I have a
secret
to whisper in your
ear.
It's a very special
secret—
the best you'll
ever hear.

It's a secret you must treasure.
It brings a great reward.
It fills your life with pleasure.
It's a promise from the Lord.
It's a secret just for children,
and it's absolutely true.
It's a secret straight from Jesus
made especially for you.

You must openly receive it.
You must keep it in your heart.
You must learn it and believe it.
That's the most important part.

Here's the secret —listen to me
for I cannot tell again:
Obey your Mom and Daddy
and the Lord will bless you, friend.

Thinking it Over

COTTON FINDS A CAVE

What did Cotton do?
What did Cotton learn?
Say this: I WILL OBEY MY
      MOMMY/ DADDY/ PARENTS

JONAH AND THE BIG FISH

Why did Jonah hide from God?
What happened after he obeyed and
went to Nineveh?
Say this: I WILL OBEY EVEN
      WHEN I DON'T FEEL LIKE IT.

Two Sons

How were these two boys different?
What did the obedient son get
    that the disobedient son didn't?
Say this: GOD REWARDS ME
    WHEN I OBEY HIM

Psst. I Have a Secret

What's the secret?
What happens when we obey our
    Mommy/ Daddy/ Parents?
Say this: GOD BLESSES ME
    WHEN I OBEY MY
    MOMMY/ DADDY/
    PARENTS.

CHAPTER SIX:
Kindness & Sympathy

T hough the world often views kindness as naive or weak, the Bible describes it as an unconquerable source of transforming power. It can change the course of the most heated argument, make enemies friends, and put hostile nations at peace.

Even the tiniest acts of kindness can become "eternal moments," life-changing occurrences that leave a person perpetually renewed. One such moment was forever engraved in my own spirit over twenty years ago by a man I hardly knew. I'm certain he has no idea of the impact for good that his one, small, spontaneous act of kindness had on another person. It will be with me till I die and then, I pray, I'll have the chance to properly thank him for it. Until then, wherever you are, Mr. Decker, I gratefully dedicate this chapter to you.

147

THE LION & THE MOUSE

The frightened little mouse
wished he'd never left his house
as the hungry lion held him tight.

"Yum, yum," the lion roared
as he studied and adored
the frightened mouse he'd eat tonight.

"Please, sir," the poor mouse cried,
"if you'll let me go then I'd
be thankful all my whole life through.

"And, someday, who knows when
well, we just might meet again,
and I will offer help to you."

The lion sighed, "Dear rat,
I've enjoyed our little chat.
But my tummy waits impatiently.

"Be a good mouse and hold still.
I'm so hungry I feel ill,
and you're just the perfect meal for me."

"But wait!" the poor mouse said,
"why not let me go instead?
You never know what you may need.

"Even though I'm very small,
I might be the one to call
and prove to be a friend indeed."

Well, the lion laughed and roared
louder than he had before.
Why, he laughed until his tail turned blue.

"What help could you give me?
You're no bigger than a flea.
What could I ever need from you?"

Even so, he let him go.
Just why he didn't know.
But soon he was so glad he had.

For before the sun had set
he was trapped inside a net,
and was feeling very
scared and sad.

Just then, the mouse appeared
and said, "No need to fear.
I'll have you free in just a bit."

The lion smiled with hope
as the mouse chewed through the rope
and freed the frightened lion of it.

They hugged and gave high fives,
both thrilled to be alive,
and thankful for a brand new friend.

They had chosen to be kind,
to leave evil thoughts behind—
a choice I highly recommend.

ONE KIND DEED

One kind deed inspires another. Like Jesus, we should be initiators of kindness.

A kind deed is like a seed
    you plant inside the heart.
Then from that tiny seed
    a Tree of Happiness soon starts.
That tree grows fast and strong.
    Soon it stretches the mind,
which makes the mouth
    say all the sweetest words that it can find.
Those words the mouth speaks forward
    plant a dozen more new seeds.
Yes, a forest full of blessings
    always starts with one kind deed.

KING KONG & KING KIND

King Kong and King Kind
    (that's King Kong's younger
    brother)
were opposites from birth
    (according to their mother).
Both were strong and hairy
    (as giant apes should be),
but in all other ways
    they lived life
      quite differently.

Kong was quite the bully
always wanting things his way.
Kind was nice and peaceful and
would always say, "Okay."

Kong was always growling.
Screams are what he most preferred.
Kind would always answer softly
using sweet and loving words.

Kong liked crushing houses or swatting down airplanes.
He loved to tear up bridges or derail a passing train.

Kind would fix these houses,
and catch the planes that fell.
He'd mend the bridges, save the trains,
and this Kind did quite well.

Kong liked hitting others and tearing up their toys.
He loved to climb on buildings and frighten girls and boys.

Kind liked hugging better and kept toys in good shape.
He loved to make kids laugh. He was a very silly ape.

Everyone for miles around greatly
loved King Kind.
But, if they had a choice in it,
they'd leave King Kong behind.
Me too and you would also.
Do correct me if I'm wrong.
Wouldn't you prefer to be King Kind
and not King Kong?

Thinking it Over

THE LION AND THE MOUSE

What did the lion want to do with
 the mouse?
How did the mouse return the kind
 deed to the lion?
Say this: I WILL DO GOOD TO
OTHERS.

KING KONG & KING KIND

What were King Kong and King
 Kind like?
Who would you rather invite to you
 birthday party?
Say this: I WILL TREAT OTHERS
 WITH KINDNESS.

One Kind Deed

Tell me about something kind
    someone has done for you.
How did this make you feel?
Say this: WHEN I'M KIND TO
OTHERS IT HELPS THEM
BE KIND TO ME.

CHAPTER SEVEN:
Perseverance &
Diligence

O ur children are growing up in a society of
instant information and service. They watch
us pull cold hard cash out of a machine on
a whim, purchase expensive items on credit, and fax
papers to the other side of the world in less than a
minute. We can clap to turn our lights on, start our
cars with a push of a button, and surf from channel
to channel without ever leaving our comfortable
seats. Success and affluence can appear to be pretty
easy from our children's point of view.

Think about it. When is the last time your
children have seen you break a sweat?

We, as parents, must always keep in mind
that our children will one day have to face life
without us. We will have done them a terrible
injustice if we fail to train them up knowing the
meaning, need and value of a little good old-
fashioned "elbow grease" and "stick-to-it-ness" every
now and then. Life is tough. It takes tenacity but it
is well worth the effort.

The Turtle & the Rabbit

Skippy was a fast,
little rabbit.
Racing was his love
and his habit.

Tazzle was a turtle with a shell.
Tazzle couldn't run very well.

Skippy challenged Tazzle to a race
knowing he would finish in first place.
Tazzle knew he'd never match Skip's speed
Still, for fun, the slow turtle agreed.

Skippy left poor Tazzle far behind
then stopped beside a tree and reclined.
"No hurry," Skippy bragged with a grin
so absolutely sure that he would win.

Tazzle jogged without stopping to rest.
Win or lose he always did his best.
Soon he passed the rabbit, don't you know?
And had only a few steps to go.

The rabbit woke up shocked and dismayed.
He never should have played or delayed.

He rushed. He tripped. He fell on his face.
And finished the race in second place!

THE ANT AND THE GRASSHOPPER

There once was a grasshopper.
Let's call him Ed.
Ed had a friend that we'll call Fred.
Fred was an ant who worked all day.
Ed, on the other hand, only played.

Fred stacked leaves all through the Spring.
Ed did not do anything.
Well, I'll admit, that's not all true—
these are the things Ed chose to do:
Swing on flowers,
chat with bugs,
play cards with a slug named Doug,
build mud castles,
watch cartoons,
stay in bed till half past noon.
Ed just did what he thought fun.
Fred toiled until the day was done.

In the Summer Fred worked hard
building homes in people's yards.
And when the owners crushed his town
Fred built a new place one shrub down.

And talk about good exercise—
Fred hauled things three times his size!
Fred liked work and did it well
then rested when the evening fell.

Ed did not like
    work at all
not in the Summer,
    Spring or Fall.
He'd watch Fred
    work every day
And wonder why
    he never played.

Fred always
    warned, "One day
    you'll see
that you have
    acted foolishly."
But Ed just
    laughed, "You're
    crazy, Fred
to work when you
    could play instead."

Then winter came
    with lots of snow,
and poor Ed had no
    place to go.
No wood to burn.
    No food to eat.
No boots to warm
    his freezing feet.

His belly growled.
    His body ached.
And soon poor Ed
    began to shake.
"I've got to find my
    good friend, Fred.
He'll keep warm and
    dry and fed."

But when he knocked
        on Fred's front door
he heard what he
        ignored before:
"I hate to say
        'I told you so'
while you stand there
        in the snow.

But what I said
        has now come true
and I cannot
        take care of you.
Don't think I'm mean,
        as you can see
I only have
        enough for me."

Ed spent the winter
        cold and sad
without the things
        he could've had.
If he had only
        had his fun
After all his
        work was done.

A high-ranking politician remarked, "If something isn't working, we must have the courage to quit." The comment struck many Americans as odd and weak-willed. "Why link courage with giving up?" we wondered and yet it was received with thunderous applause. Perseverance, it would appear, has lost some of its luster. We, as parents, citizens and educators, must work hard to change that. If we do not, our children will grow up in a world of "courageous quitters" and that would be sad indeed. Start simple. Then diligently persevere. Here's one to begin that journey with.

"QUITTER THROWFITTER"

Quitter Throwfitter
was not a go-getter.
In fact, he was more
of a pouter and hitter.
A kicker. A screamer.
A fit-throwing-flurry.
Quitter would quit
all he tried in a hurry.

His mom tried to teach
     him to tie his shoes.
She showed exactly
     what to do.
He watched and listened,
     then blurted with joy,
"I can do it myself! I'm a
     very big boy!"

He grabbed the shoelaces
     and tied them up tight,
then looked to his
     mother to see her delight.
"Good try!" she said,
     "tell me what you forgot."
Quitter had tied his
     shoestrings into knots.

"I'll never be able to tie
     my own shoes!"
He shouted and screamed
     and stomped and brewed.
"I quit! I quit! I won't
     try anymore!"
He yanked off his shoes
     and then ran out the door.

Speaking of
running, Quitter
loved to race,
but only if he
could come in
first place.
The minute
Quitter fell one
step behind
he'd be a poor
sport of the
crankiest kind.

"I quit! I quit!"
he'd fuss at
his friends.
"I'm not going
to race if I
can't win!"

He'd wail and
whimper and
fall to the
ground,
and whine till
no friends were
left around.

188

Quitter's
  throwfitters
  did not
  help one bit.
Indeed, they did
  just the
  opposite.

His mother told
  Quitter to
  stay in his
  room
if all he
  could do was
  to fuss and
  fume.

His attitude got
  so ugly and
  mean
none of his
  friends
  wanted him
  on their
  team.

"I've got to do better. I can't always quit.
Only a baby's supposed to throw fits.
I've got to keep trying and stop giving in!
I should keep trying then try, try again."

From that moment on Quitter did what he said.
When he felt like quitting, he went on instead.
Now he is able to tie his own shoes
and doesn't get mad if he happens to lose.

Do you give up easily? Do you throw big fits?
Do you get frustrated and fall down and quit?
Then pick yourself up and stick out your chin,
brush yourself off and then try, try again.

Thinking it Over

The Turtle and the Rabbit

Which animal is really faster?
Why, then, did the faster rabbit los
     to the much slower turtle?
Say this: WIN OR LOSE, I WILL
     ALWAYS DO MY BEST.

The Ant and the Grasshopper

What can we learn from Fred the Ant?
What can we learn from Ed the
     Grasshopper?
Say This: I WILL BE A HARD,
     HAPPY WORKER.

QUITTER THROWFITTER

What did Quitter do after he tied his shoestrings into knots?
How did Quitter finally learn to tie them correctly?
Say this: I'LL ALWAYS KEEP TRYING TILL I LEARN.

CHAPTER SEVEN:
Courage

Courage comes in all shapes and sizes. There is the dramatic level of courage that enabled Joan of Arc to stare death in the face and there is the much less dramatic, though still courageous, quiet story of the five-year-old girl who admits to breaking her mother's priceless heirloom.

A child needs courage to say "no" when all of his friends are screaming "yes"; courage to be uniquely themselves instead of a social clone; courage to believe when all those around them doubt; courage to speak the truth even when it may mean personal discomfort; and, many, regularly call on courage to help them stay in beds once the lights go off.

Our children need to know that when life isn't easy it is manageable with courage.

DAVID & GOLIATH

Ha! Ha! Ha!" Goliath sneered.
Strong and mean and ten feet tall.
"Send a man to come and fight me
Or we'll kill you one and all."

"I have muscles!
    Big, strong
    muscles!
See my sword?
    See my spear?
Send a man to come
    and fight me!
Just one man who
    doesn't fear."

"I'm Goliath! Warrior! Champion!"
He growled with an evil glare.
"Send a man to come and fight me!
Come and fight me if you dare!"

Ev'ry morning. Ev'ry evening.
Ev'ry day for forty days.
Goliath stood and screamed and challenged.
But all Saul's soldiers were afraid.

"Surely there is someone (with you)
who will fight me face to face."
Goliath sighed with great impatience.
"If you win — we'll be your slaves!"

Not one man in King Saul's army
dared to step across and fight.
"Scaredycats!" Goliath taunted.
"Send one man or die tonight!"

Then a shepherd boy named David
walked straight up before the King,
"I will fight this big-mouthed giant!
And I'll kill him with my sling!"

"Y-you will kill him?" King Saul stammered.
"You are brave but much too small.
And this slingshot, my dear child,
will never make Goliath fall."

"Well?" Goliath stood and thundered
as he sharpened up his sword.
"I laugh at Saul and his whole army
and the God that you call 'Lord'!"

David's heart beat fast inside him.
"No one talks of God like that!
Let me at him!" David shouted.
"Let me knock this giant flat!"

"Very well," King Saul spoke slowly,
"You're the only hope we've got.
Sling it fast and straight, small warrior;
you may only get one shot."

Every eye was on young David
as he bent to gather stones.
"Lord, I know that You are with me
guiding every stone that's thrown."

"What is this?" Goliath wondered.
Why, he nearly flipped his lid!
"This is who will kill Goliath?!
This small, skinny, runty kid?!"

Goliath's face turned red with fury
as he raised his shiny spear.
"I'll feed you to the birds
and to the beasts who've gathered here!"

But David wasn't frightened
by the giant's spear or sword.
"You're the birdseed!" David answered,
"For this battle is the Lord's!"

The big giant steamed and snorted
while the soldiers watched spellbound.
David loaded up his slingshot
and spun it 'round and 'round.

Then whoosh! faster than a bullet
David's rock whizzed straight ahead,
and before Goliath knew it
he was falling . . . spinning . . . dead.

My five-year-old's eyes light up when I begin this story. There is a subtle lesson in this one as well: Choose your friends carefully. If they are of strong faith and character, chances are you will be, too.

SHADRACH, MESHACH, & ABEDNEGO

King Nebuchadnezzar built a huge statue made of pure gold.

"Gather all my leaders together," he commanded.

Once the people arrived King Nebuchadnezzar said, "See this big statue? He is our new god."

"He's beautiful!" one of his leaders yelled from the crowd.

"Breathtaking!" added another.

"He's the most awesome god I have seen all week!" still another called out.

The King then said, "When the music starts, fall on your knees and bow down. If you do not bow down and worship," he said, "I shall throw you into the fiery furnace."

Suddenly the whole hillside was filled with loud and strange music. The large crowd fell to its knees and bowed down before the lifeless statue.

Just then, a couple of the king's leaders peeked and saw three young men standing in the crowd.

"I don't believe it," said the first.

"The nerve!" replied the second.

"Let's tattle!" they agreed.

"Your Majesty!" they screamed and pointed. "These men are not obeying you."

"Bring them to me now!" demanded the King.

They were three of the king's wisest leaders. Their names were Shadrach, Meshach, and Abednego. King Nebuchadnezzar pressed his face into theirs.

"I will give you one more chance. If you'll bow down now, I'll let you go. If you do not, I will throw you into the furnace." The King laughed, "No god can save you from me."

"Your Majesty," the three began, "the God we serve can not only save us from you, O King, but from your furnace of fire as well."

Then before Nebuchadnezzar could answer, they added, "but even if our God doesn't, we still will not worship this gold statue."

Nebuchadnezzar's face twisted with rage. "Heat it up seven times hotter!" he shouted. "And bring me my strongest soldiers to tie these men up!" Nebuchadnezzar stomped his feet and screamed, "Do it now!"

Immediately, the king's strongest soldiers tied Shadrach, Meshach, and Abednego and threw them into the furnace. The fire was so hot that some flames leaped out and instantly killed the soldiers.

Nebuchadnezzar gasped and sprang to his feet. "Didn't we throw only three men into the fire?"

"Yes, Your Majesty," the people stuttered, "T-T-Three."

"But there are four now!" the king gulped, "and the fourth one looks like a god!"

Nebuchadnezzar tiptoed closer to the furnace and called the young men to come out. Everyone crowded around them.

"They're not burnt at all!" one man shouted.
"They do not even smell like smoke!" said another.

King Nebuchadnezzar said, "Praises to the God of Shadrach, Meshach, and Abednego who rescued them from the fire! He is powerful and should be worshiped!"

The King bragged about their great faith and courage and gave them even greater positions of leadership in his kingdom.

Thinking it Over

DAVID & GOLIATH

How did all Saul's soldiers feel about Goliath?
Why did David feel differently?
Say this: I WILL BE BRAVE WHEN BIG CHALLENGES
           COME MY WAY.*
(Note : You may want to talk about an upcoming Doctor visit, Dentist appointment, new social situation, new school, athletic tryouts, auditions, etc.)

SHADRACH, MESHACH, & ABEDNEGO

Why did Shadrach, Meshach, and Abednego refuse
    to bow down?

What happened in the end?

Say this: I WILL PLEASE GOD EVEN
    WHEN OTHERS DON'T.

CHAPTER NINE:
Companionship & Example

T here are many great stories of noble persons our children should know by heart. I have purposefully focused on only two: the first Adam and the last Adam.

The first Adam is the male half of the world's most famous couple. His story is not inspirational and his legacy a constant source of grief. Of course, the story would have been just as disappointing if it would've been Andy (that's me) and Eve. The Bible makes that clear when it reminds us in Romans 3:23 that "all have sinned and fall short of the glory of God."

However, thankfully, the story didn't end with the first Adam but, rather, with the last. Paul says in 1 Corinthians 15:45: "Thus it is written, 'The first man Adam became a living being"; the last Adam became a life-giving spirit.'"

Ultimately, we will be imitating one or the other. The first Adam chose his own way and paid for it with his life. The last Adam chose God's way and was highly exalted. (see Philippians 2:9).

ADAM & EVE

Adam and Eve lived happily in a beautiful garden. They had ponds to swim in. They had meadows to run through. They had trees to climb on and to get food from.

"You may eat the fruit from all of the trees but this one," said God. "The fruit from this tree will make you die."

One day Eve met a talking snake.

"Eat this fruit and you will be as smart as God," said the snake.

"But if I eat it I will die," said Eve.

"Don't be silly," said the snake. "You won't die."

Eve took a bite of the fruit and so did Adam.

"I don't feel so good," said Eve.

"Me neither," said Adam.

"Ha ha ha," said the snake. "I tricked you."

"We should not have believed the snake," said Eve. "We should have believed God," said Adam. They were very sad.

Adam and Eve had to leave the beautiful garden. They lived for many years and then, just as God had said, they died.

A long, long time ago
in a tiny crib of hay,
a baby boy was born
on what became
a special day.
The baby's name
was Jesus.
His mother's name
was Mary.
His father's name
was Joseph.
They were plain
and ordinary.
His father
was a builder;
he made things
out of wood.
Jesus worked
beside His dad
and did the best
He could.

JESUS, SON OF GOD

He watched His father closely
then copied ev'ry stroke.
They were kind and honest.
They were simple, gentlefolk.

Jesus loved His parents.
He did the things they asked.
He helped without complaining.
He worked hard at His tasks.

Soon Jesus was a man.
He helped the weak and poor.
He fed all those who hungered
     with the power of the Lord.

He healed those with diseases.
He made blind people see.
He made the lame to walk again
     and set the whole world free.

Jesus loved
    the children.
    He said, "I want
    them near."
He stood one
    in the middle
    then said for
    all to hear:

"You'll never
    taste of
    Heaven.
    No, you'll not
    know the joy
unless you once
    again become
    a little girl or
    boy.

The greatest in
    God's kingdom
    are not the strong
    and tall.
Instead they are the
    childlike—
    the tender and
    the small."

Jesus was a wonder.
The kindest man who lived.
Whenever someone hurt Him,
    Jesus would forgive.

Jesus loved all people,
    but not all loved Him back.
Some hated Him, and secretly,
    they planned a mean attack.

They said,
   "He is a liar!"
They shouted,
   "He must die!"
They put Him on a
   wooden cross,
   wrapped thorns
   above His eyes.

They laughed at Him
   and teased Him.
   They called
   Him ugly names.
They said that He
   was not God's
   Son as He had
   claimed.

But Jesus didn't
   hate them. He
   loved them
   through and
   through.
He said, "Dear God,
   forgive them.
   They know not
   what they do."

It was a very
   sad day, for
   soon Jesus
   was dead.
And even those
   who were His
   friends all ran
   away and fled.

They put Him in a
   grave site
   carved deep
   inside a hill.
And for the next
   three days
   Lord Jesus
   lay there still.

Then in a burst
   of glory,
   to everyone's
   surprise,
Jesus came alive
   again and
   opened up
   His eyes.

All His friends
    were happy
    to see His
    lovely face.
His eyes were
    sweet and
    tender. His
    words so full
    of grace.

He said He had to
    go, for His
    task on earth
    was done.
The work of those
    He left behind
    had only
    just begun.

He said to tell the
    whole world
    of God's great
    love and care.
He promised to be
    watching
    and listening
    to their prayers.

He said they should
        believe in Him
        and do the
        things He taught,
to love the Lord with
        all their hearts
        and keep Him in
        their thoughts.

For God so loved
        the world
        that He sent His
        only Son
to die upon the cross
        for the sins of
        everyone."

Then Jesus went
  up in the sky
  to sit at God's
  right hand.
He had pleased
  the Lord
  by doing
  everything
  He'd planned.

He promised to
  come back
  again. I can't
  wait for that
  day!
He'll gather those
  who love Him,
  who trust Him
  and obey.

Thinking it Over

ADAM & EVE

What were Adam and Eve not allowed to do?
What happened after they disobeyed?
Say this: GOD'S COMMANDS ALWAYS PROTECT
    AND BLESS ME

Jesus, Son of God

How did Jesus treat others?
How does God want us to treat others?
Say this: I WILL LOVE OTHERS JUST
 LIKE JESUS DID.

CHAPTER TEN:
Respect &
Reverence

Jesus said, "You shall love your neighbor as yourself."

The "as yourself" part is worth special notice. How are we to love others? As we love ourselves. Indeed, it is impossible to love others while hating ourselves. The same is true when it comes to the area of respect.

One of the surest ways to teach our children to respect others is to first respect them. We show our respect for them (or our lack of respect) primarily through our words, our tone, and our actions. Respect, like so many things in training up our children, is more often "caught" than "taught." This is also true in teaching our children to respect and revere God.

Be on your best behavior. Little eyes are always watching and little ears are always listening.

237

SASSY

Sassy was a little girl
who talked in hateful tones.
Her words came out like lightning
and chilled you to the bone.

238

She sassed all of her uncles,
her aunts, her mom, her dad.
She even sassed her grandmother!
Now that is really bad!

She sassed all of her schoolmates.
She sassed her teachers, too.
She sassed so much her parents
didn't know quite what to do.

Then one day Sassy's Dad said,
"I have a plan to try.
I'll need a tape recorder
And here's the reason why.

When Sassy hears how ugly
Her speech so often sounds
that just might be the cure
that will turn our girl around."

So that's just what they did.
They recorded all she said,
then played it for her every night
before she went to bed.

At first she thought, "That's funny."
But when she'd listened more,
she soon felt more embarrassed
than she'd ever felt before.

"I can't believe I said that.
I sound so rude and mean."
She hid under the covers
so she could not be seen.

She sobbed, "I am so sorry.
How ugly I have been!
I promise I will never talk
like that ever again."

Sassy kept her promise.
Her words are oh so sweet.
Now Sassy is the kindest girl
that you could ever meet.

This is a song I learned as a very young child in church. We always sang it slowly and in a soft voice. It nurtured in me a sense of reverence for God and his awesomeness, and it gave me a feeling of worth that, somehow, this great, big, powerful God would allow me to come into His presence and sit. I later discovered it is simply a verse from the Bible put to music. You'll find it in the tiny book of Habakkuk, chapter two, verse twenty.

LET ALL THE EARTH KEEP SILENT

The Lord is in
His holy temple.
Let all the earth keep
silence before Him.
Keep silence.
Keep silence.
Keep silence before Him.

PITIFUL PENELOPE

Penelope was impolite.
She'd snort.
She'd slurp.
She'd spit.

She'd snap,
"Move over, Charlie!
Make room!
I'm gonna sit!"

She'd eat in front of others
  and stuff her mouth with food.
She'd smack her lips and burp out loud
  which, of course, is rude.

She'd cut in line. She'd interrupt.
She'd twiddle with her gum.
She'd pull it out and suck it in
     and wrap it 'round her thumb.
She'd click her heels. She'd pick her teeth.
She'd even pick her nose.
She'd never use a tissue.
She'd wipe it on her clothes.

She'd never say, "Why, thank you!",
    "Excuse me," "Would you please?"
She treated people like they had some
        terrible disease.

She'd take the best seat on the bus,
and she would never share.
She'd always win the games she played
but never fair and square.

She got all that she
wanted—oh,
well, that all depends;
every *thing* but not a
single, solitary friend.

Thinking it Over

Sassy

What was Sassy's problem?
How do harsh or ugly words
    make others feel?
Say this: I WILL SPEAK WITH
    GENTLENESS AND
    RESPECT.

Let All the Earth Keep Silent

Can you think of something you've seen
    that amazed you so much your
    mouth dropped open and you
    couldn't say anything but "wow!"?
Let's sit still and think about how
    powerful and awesome God is.
Say this: GOD IS AMAZING

PITIFUL PENELOPE

What are some of the bad behaviors
    Penelope had?
How might those bad behaviors
    effect others?
Say this: I WILL BE CONSIDERATE
    OF OTHERS AND PRACTICE
    GOOD MANNERS.